Look c

Written by Jo Windsor
Illustrated by Dave Gunson

“Look at me,”
said the alien.

"I am
in the backyard."

"Look at me,"
said the alien.

"I am
in the tree."

"Look at me,"
said the alien.

"Look at me."

“Look at me,”
said the alien.

"I am
in the mud!"

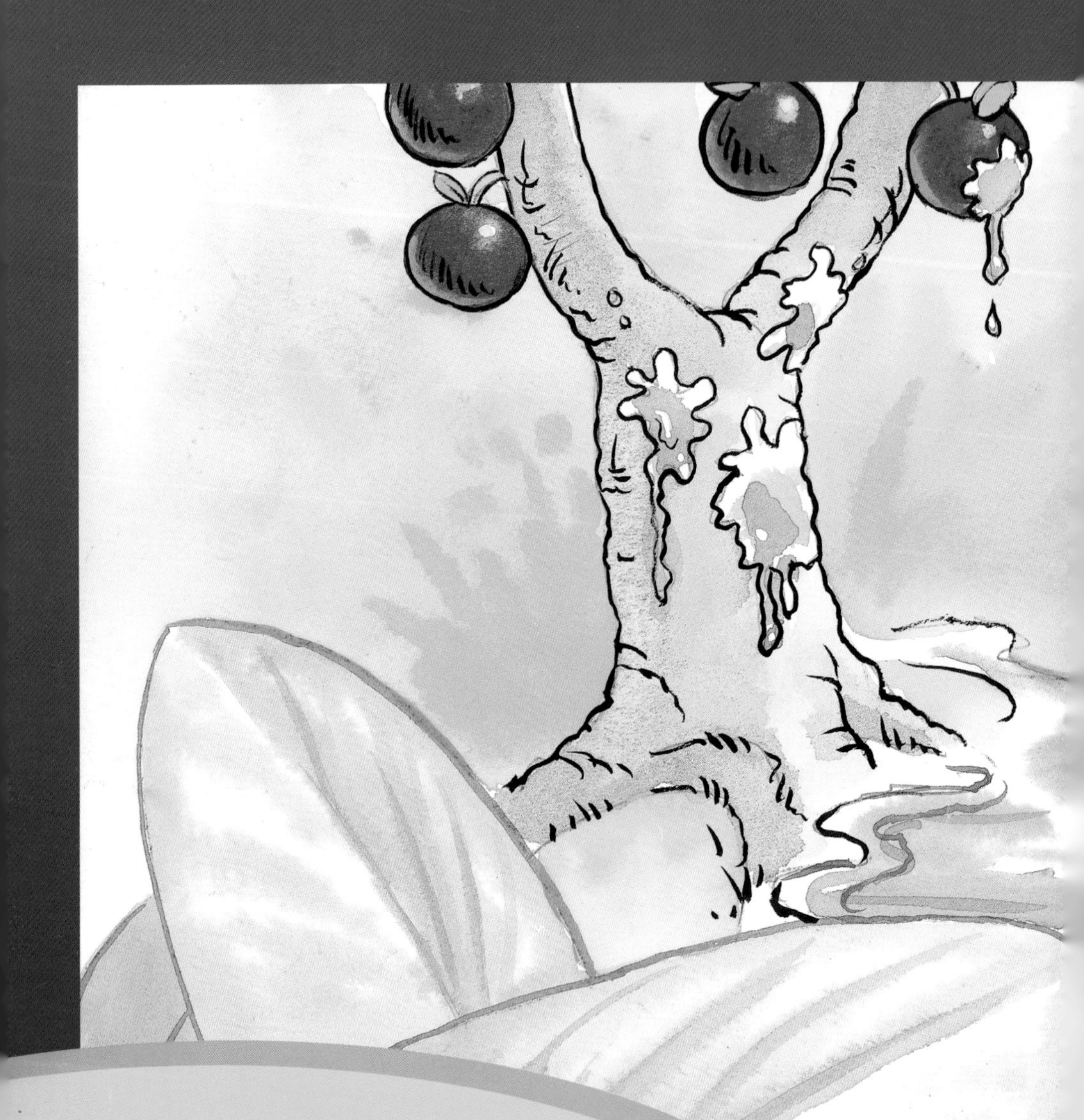

“Look at me,”
said the alien.

"Look at me."

“Look at me,”
said the alien.

"I am
in the bathtub."

A Story Sequence

1

2

3
4

Guide Notes

Title: Look at Me!
Stage: Emergent – Magenta
Genre: Fiction
Approach: Guided Reading
Processes: Thinking Critically, Exploring Language, Processing Information
Written and Visual Focus: Story Sequence
Word Count: 62

Forming the Foundation

Tell the children that the story is about an alien who finds himself in a new place and goes out to explore it.
Talk to them about what is on the front cover. Read the title and the author/illustrator.
"Walk" through the book, focusing on the illustrations and talking to the children about each situation the alien finds himself in.
Leave pages 12-13 for prediction.

Read the text together.

Thinking Critically

(sample questions)

After the reading
- Why do you think the alien keeps saying, "Look at me."?
- What do you think the alien might do after his bath?

Exploring Language

(ideas for selection)

Terminology
Title, cover, author, illustrator, illustrations

Vocabulary
Interest words: alien, tree, mud
High-frequency words: look, at, me, said, the, I, am
Positional word: in